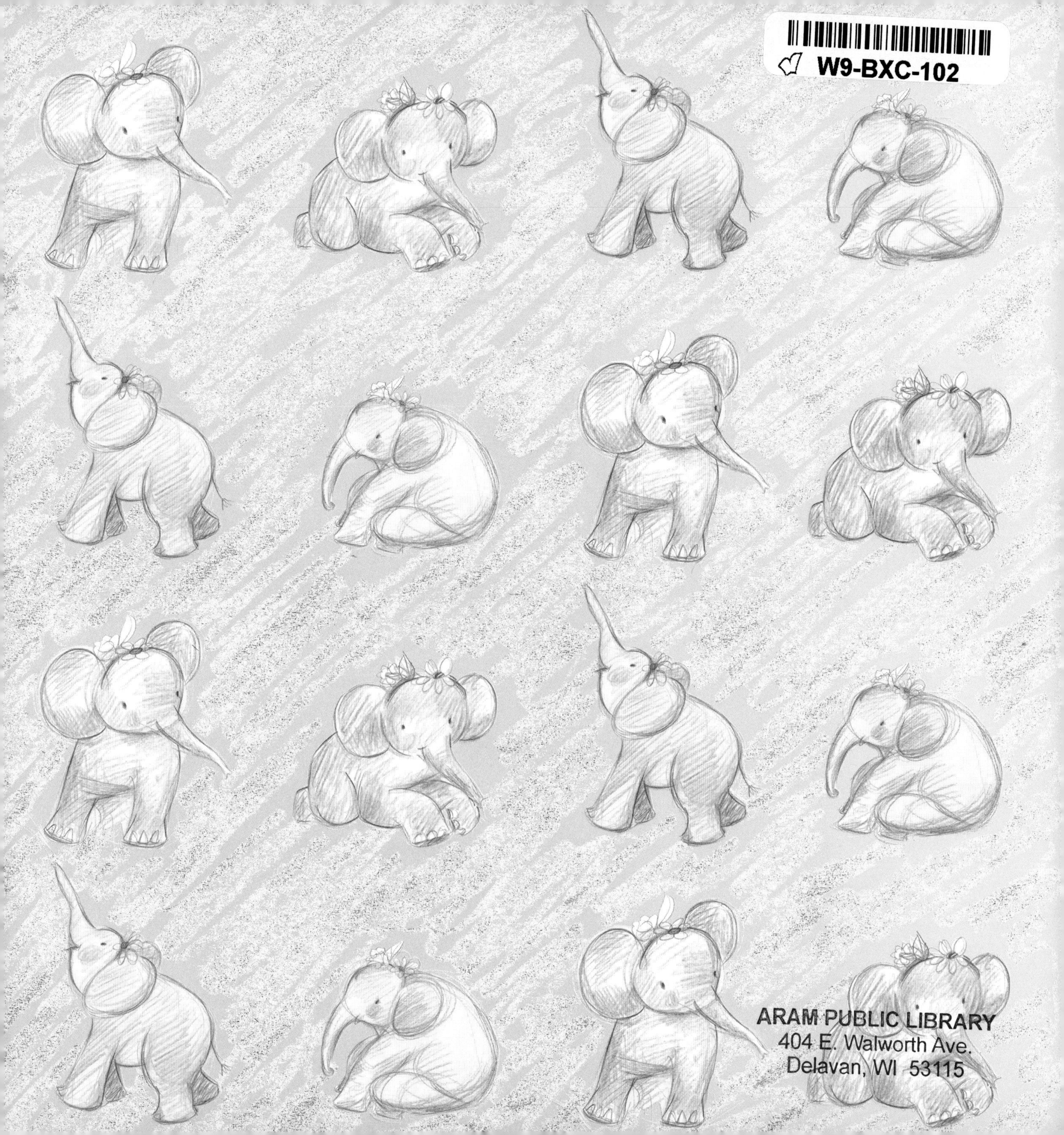

For kids with colorful imaginations

—A.F.

To my sons, Hudson and Ryder,
and to my beautiful niece, Cru

—C.L.

little bee books

An imprint of Bonnier Publishing Group
853 Broadway, New York, New York 10003

Manufactured in China LEO 1015
First Edition 10 9 8 7 6 5 4 3 2 1
Library of Congress Cataloging-in-Publication Data
is available upon request.
ISBN 978-1-4998-0156-9
littlebeebooks.com
bonnierpublishing.com

Lucy and Lila

by Alison Fletcher

illustrated by Christopher Lyles

little bee books

The day was almost over as Lucy skipped into her last class.

"I love Art!" she said excitedly. "Hi, Ms. Martin!"

"Hello, Lucy. Good afternoon, everyone!" announced Ms. Martin. "Please take your seats so we can get started."

“Today, I’d like each of you to draw pictures of what you did last weekend,” said Ms. Martin. “You may use crayons, colored pencils, or markers.”

Lucy thought about her weekend, and a big smile spread over her face.

"But I had the most boring weekend EVER," said Joey.
"I don't know what to draw."

"Oh, come on now. I'm sure you can think of something," said Ms. Martin.

Joey struggled with his drawing.

But Lucy, on the other hand, knew exactly what she was going to draw!

And once she started drawing, she couldn't stop! She even needed more paper.

Stacey looked over at Lucy's drawings.
"Ms. Martin said you're supposed to draw pictures from your weekend—not your imagination."

"I *am* drawing pictures from my weekend," replied Lucy.

"Is that from a movie or something?" asked Joey.

Stacey and Joey started to giggle.

"Okay, finish up, everyone," said Ms. Martin.
"I want each of you to present your work to the class."

Stacey showed everyone pictures
from her princess party.

Billy showed the class drawings
of his new puppy, Clyde.

Joey had just one
drawing to show.

“Okay, who’s next? Lucy?”

Lucy ran to the front of the class and described her weekend. "Last weekend I met a new friend. Her name is Lila."

Lucy held up a drawing of a pink elephant. Everyone started giggling.

"Lucy, is Lila your new toy?"

"No, Ms. Martin," said Lucy.
"Lila is a REAL elephant."
The other students laughed
and snickered, but Lucy continued.

"Lila and I had a great time together. We played Frisbee in the yard. . . .

And we chased butterflies through the meadow."

“We played hide-and-seek in the garden. . . .

And we played on the swings.”

"We picked apples from the orchard. . . .

And then we had
a tea party by the stream.

It was the BEST day ever!"

"Hey, Ms. Martin?" interrupted Joey. "I forgot to show everyone something. Here's a drawing of the blue dinosaur I met yesterday!"

The class roared with laughter.

"What's so funny?" asked Lucy. "I'm NOT making this up."

“Class, settle down. And Lucy,”
said Ms. Martin with a wink,
“I hope we can all meet Lila one day.”

Suddenly the bell rang, and it was time to go home. Everyone put away their supplies and gathered in their bus lines.

"Great work today, kids," said Ms. Martin.
"I'll see you next week."

On the bus ride home, the kids were talking about their drawings.
When Lucy's stop came up, Joey called out to her.
"Hey Lucy, have fun with your green elephant!"

"She's pink, and you're NOT funny," said Lucy.
Lucy knew that everyone was laughing at her, but she didn't care.

Lucy watched as the bus pulled away. She could see Joey laughing at her through the window.

But then, a big, pink trunk wrapped around her and gave her a huge hug.

“I knew you’d be here!” said Lucy.

"Are you ready to play, Lila?
Come on, let's go!"

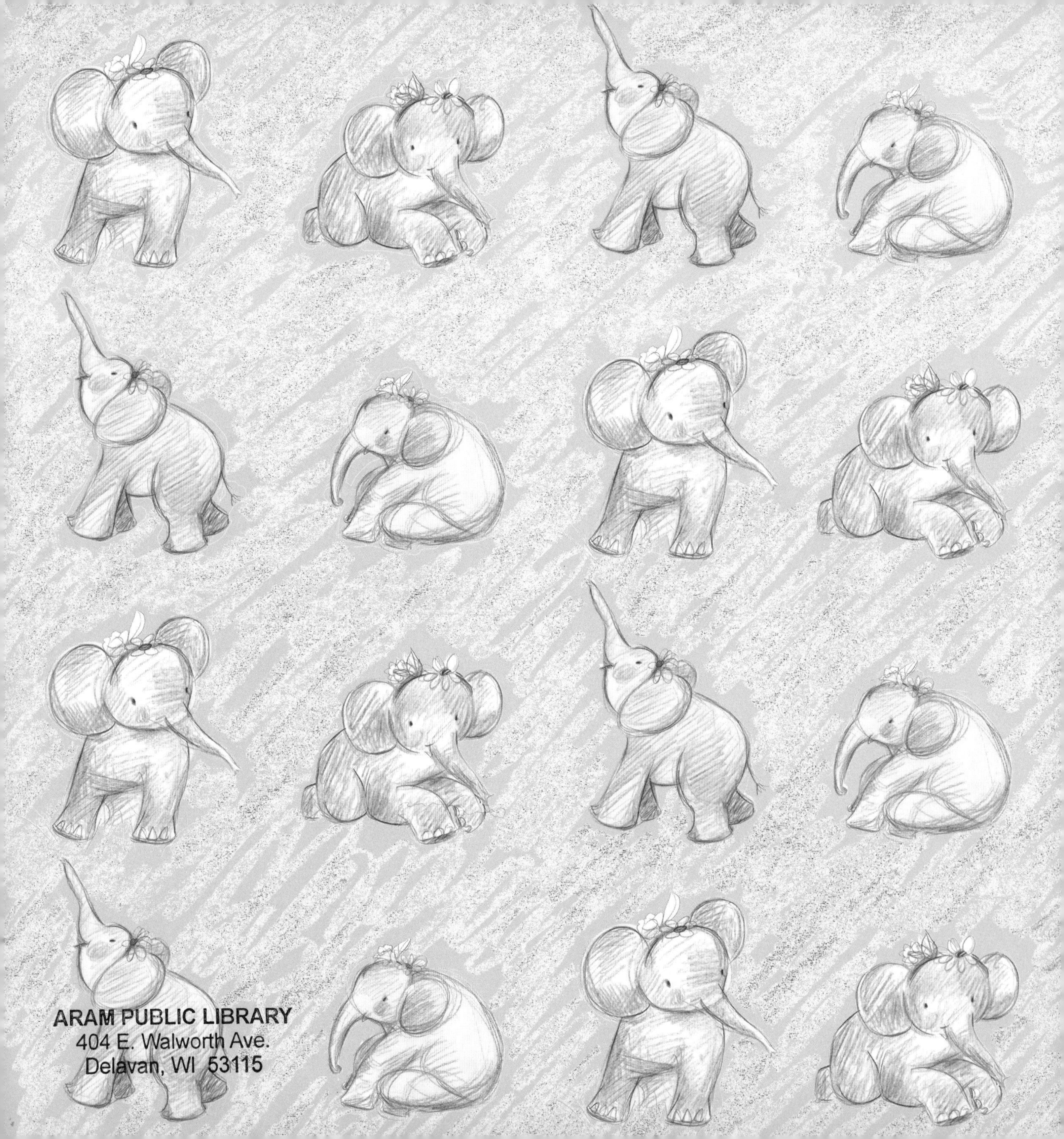